The Christmas Sheep
and Other Stories

With especial thanks to Leslie Guest

A.R.

For Anthony

R.M.

The CHRISTMAS SHEEP
and Other Stories

Avril Rowlands

Illustrated by
Rosslyn Moran

LION
Children's Books

Text copyright © 2000 Avril Rowlands
Illustrations copyright © 2000 Rosslyn Moran
This edition copyright © 2000 Lion Publishing

The moral rights of the author and illustrator
have been asserted

Published by
Lion Publishing plc
Sandy Lane West, Oxford, England
www.lion-publishing.co.uk
ISBN 0 7459 4553 8

First edition 2000
10 9 8 7 6 5 4 3 2 1 0

Acknowledgments
These stories have been adapted from *The Animals'*
Christmas and Other Stories, 1997, also from
Lion Publishing. 'The Christmas Sheep' was originally
called 'The Lonely Sheep', and 'The Confused Camels'
was called 'The Camels Who Went Round in Circles'.

A catalogue record for this book is available
from the British Library

Typeset in 14/22 Garamond ITC Lt BT
Printed and bound in Singapore

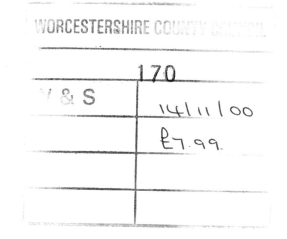

Contents

To Begin...

There is a legend that, on the first Christmas night, animals knelt before the crib at Bethlehem to worship the newborn king. Perhaps they understood more than many people at that time, and perhaps there are things that animals can show us now about Christmas…

The Donkey Makes a Choice

Two donkeys plodded along a dusty road towards town. They were tired and walked slowly. Heavy baskets were strapped to their sides.

'My baskets are heavier than usual,' grumbled Ezra. 'And one is heavier than the other.'

Moses said nothing. His baskets were heavy too, but he did not complain.

'You'd think that they could have filled the panniers evenly,' Ezra went on. 'I'm not sure I can walk all the way to town with one side heavier than the other!'

Moses sighed. 'You know, Ezra, you must be the worst-tempered donkey in the whole of Israel.'

Ezra snorted. 'Here we are, carrying these heavy baskets to town, when we could be lazing in a field, eating clover and sweet grass, and you complain that I'm bad-tempered. What do you expect?'

'Oh, life's not so bad,' said Moses.

'It's not as if we ever get any thanks for what we do – just kicks and lashes if we don't work hard enough.'

'It could be worse,' said Moses.

Ezra snorted and they walked into Nazareth in silence.

Now, unknown to the two donkeys, the Emperor Augustus had decided to count the number of people living in the Roman Empire. Everyone was told to return to the place where they were born to register their names.

'It's good news for us, though,' Ezra's master said to his wife. '*We* don't have to travel anywhere because we were born here. But others do. People will pay a lot to hire donkeys.' He rubbed his hands. 'If we wait for a day or two, we should get a good price.'

'We might get a lot for hiring out Moses,' his wife said. 'But what about Ezra? No one would want him, he's far too bad-tempered.'

Soon, almost every donkey and horse, every mule and ox in Nazareth had been hired out. Moses was hired by a couple who were going to Jericho. He was pleased.

'I've never been so far away,' he told Ezra. 'It will be just like a holiday.'

'Some holiday!' Ezra snorted. 'You must be joking! Have you seen how big those people are?'

'Well, I'm looking forward to it,' said Moses. 'I think every donkey ought to travel at some point in his life. It'll broaden my horizons. I hope you're hired for a nice trip, Ezra.'

'Me? Huh! If anyone tries to hire me, I'll bite their hands!'

And that is just what Ezra did. Whenever anyone came near

him he tried to bite them. Soon, he was the only donkey left in Nazareth. This made him feel lonely, as he had no one to hear his grumbles. And, without Moses, he had to work harder than ever, so he grew more and more bad-tempered.

One evening, he reached his stable to find a man and a young girl waiting with his master.

'Of course I'd like you to hire him.' Then his master shook his head. 'But it's only fair to tell you that he's a nasty animal. He kicks, he bites, and he's thrown everyone who's tried to mount him.'

'We've tried everywhere else,' said the man, whose name was Joseph. 'And I must hire something. Mary's expecting a baby and she can't walk all the way to Bethlehem.' He turned to Mary. 'What do you think?'

Mary gave Ezra a long look which made him feel most uncomfortable. He turned his back on her.

'I think,' she said quietly, 'that we should talk to the donkey and ask if he'll carry me.'

Ezra was amazed. No one had ever spoken like that before. He twitched his tail and turned his head to watch. Mary walked towards him, holding out her hand.

She's a fool, Ezra thought. He opened his mouth ready to snap his teeth but, for some reason, he closed it again. Mary laid a hand on his head.

'Please,' Mary said, 'would you take us to Bethlehem? It's a long way and we'll all get very tired before we get there, but Joseph and I have to make the journey. We have no choice. But you have. You must only take us if you want to.'

Ezra moved slightly.

'Careful, Mary,' Joseph warned.

'You need only take us if you really want to,' she whispered gently in one of Ezra's long, grey ears.

Ezra didn't know why he stood quietly as Joseph lifted Mary onto his back. But he did. Mary leaned forward and stroked his neck.

'What's his name?' she asked.

'Ezra,' said his master, shaking his head once more. 'Well, I'm amazed. I've never seen him like that before.' He took the money that Joseph offered. 'I just hope it's not one of his tricks.'

Mary bent down. 'Well Ezra, shall we go?'

Ezra lowered his head, walked out of his master's stable and began the long walk to Bethlehem.

They walked until late into the night. They walked until the moon was high and the stars were out. And, as they walked, Mary talked to the donkey. She told him about her life and about an angel who had come to tell her that her baby would be special. Her baby was God's son.

Ezra listened as he walked along the rough road, picking his way carefully so that Mary should have a smooth ride.

At last they stopped and Joseph lifted Mary from Ezra's back. 'We must eat and sleep. Are you very tired?'

'Not really,' she said. She turned and kissed Ezra's nose. 'Thank you.'

Mary and Joseph fed Ezra then ate their supper in a hollow near to the road. He watched them for a while, then wandered away. Mary and Joseph were talking quietly. He could hear the murmur of their voices, a friendly sound in the empty countryside. He heard them laugh and was suddenly filled with sadness. No one, animal or person, had ever laughed with him. He watched as Mary settled herself to sleep and Joseph tucked a blanket around her.

No one, Ezra thought, from the time he had been taken from his mother, had ever been kind to him or shown him any love. He felt tears roll down his old cheeks but shook them away. Ezra never cried. He turned and suddenly realized that he was free. Free to find fields of clover and sweet grass. He turned once more to look at Mary and Joseph, now lying side by side.

But don't I owe them something? he found himself thinking. She was kind to me. She talked to me and kissed me and gave me a carrot. What will they do if I leave?

He shook his head. What's a kind voice and a gentle hand and a carrot after all? he thought. They'll manage if I leave them, they'll be all right. Someone will come along in the morning and give them a lift. They don't need me.

But still he waited.

'Think, Ezra, what it will mean if you do stay,' he said to himself. 'We get to Bethlehem, stay a day or two, then make the long journey home to Nazareth. And what lies at the end? What thanks do I get for staying? Kicks and curses and heavy loads to carry. I'll have lost my one chance of freedom!'

For a long while Ezra stood and watched Mary and Joseph as

they slept. Then he sighed and slowly returned to the hollow where they lay. Gently, he nudged Mary's shoulder with his soft nose. She stirred, but did not wake. Ezra sighed again, then stood, silently guarding them, all through the long, dark night. He had made his choice.

So Ezra, the worst-tempered donkey in the whole of Israel, plodded, without a grumble or a word of complaint, along the many miles to Bethlehem.

And in the stable in Bethlehem, he had his reward, for he was one of the first to see the miracle of Jesus' birth. And at that sight, the donkey bowed his head and cried – this time with joy.

The Christmas Sheep

One cold winter's night, three shepherds sat huddled round a fire watching over their sheep. Their flock huddled together in a corner of the sheepfold and watched the shepherds.

'All right for them,' said one of the sheep. 'Nice and cosy round that fire.'

'We could always go a bit nearer,' bleated a second sheep.

'And be shooed away? Not likely.'

A third sheep sighed. 'Who'd be a sheep? I mean, just look at us. Silly tails and small heads.'

'My head's not small,' the second sheep objected. 'And my tail's very nice.'

'Oh, come on,' jeered the third sheep. 'We look ridiculous!'

'Well, I'd rather be a sheep than one of them,' said the first sheep, nodding her head towards the shepherds.

'Do you think,' said the third sheep, 'that God made us sheep as some kind of joke? To give him a good laugh?'

'Maybe,' said the first sheep.

'But surely we were made for a reason?' said a quiet voice. It came from a small sheep standing apart from the rest.

The other sheep looked at her for a moment, then turned away.

'God may have made us sheep as some sort of joke,' said the first sheep, 'but I'm very thankful I'm not like that…' She nodded in the direction of the small sheep.

'So am I,' agreed the second sheep.

The small sheep looked at the shepherds. It must be warm by the fire, she thought. But she did not envy them. The shepherds had a hard life out in the fields.

The wind blew and the small sheep shivered. The ground was frozen and there was a nip in the air. Soon it would snow. It would be warmer huddled close to the other sheep, but she did not try to join them. If she did, they would only push her away.

From the moment she had been born she had known she was different. None of the other lambs would play with her. 'Go away,' they had said, when she had tried to join in their running and jumping games. 'We don't want you.'

'Why?' she had asked, but no one would tell her.

She had tried asking her mother, but her mother only turned away from her in silence. She had tried asking the other sheep, but they only laughed at her and called her names. So the small sheep had grown up keeping to a different side of the field. She was small because she ate only the poorest grass. The best grass was eaten by the rest of the flock.

If only the other sheep would talk to me, she thought. If only I could huddle close to them just once, instead of always being on my own.

Time passed. The flock was quiet and the shepherds slept

beside their fire. A thick white frost covered the field. It grew very dark.

Then the field was suddenly bathed in a golden light and a voice spoke out of the black night sky. The small sheep listened.

The voice stopped, the light faded, and the small sheep left the shelter of the tree and began crossing the field.

Might as well see what all the fuss is about, she thought as she jumped through a gap in the stone wall. No one will miss me.

Reuben, always a light sleeper, had also seen the light and heard the voice. He woke his companions.

'Elias! Joshua! Did you see that?'

The shepherds stirred.

'What…?' asked Joshua.

'Has someone been after the sheep?' asked Elias.

'I don't know,' said Reuben. 'I saw a light…'

Joshua looked round. 'There's no light here.'

'But there was,' Reuben said. 'And there was a voice. It spoke – about a newborn baby…'

'I heard something too,' said Elias, 'but I thought I was dreaming. After all, what would someone be doing in the middle of the night, in the middle of a field, in the middle of winter, talking about a newborn baby? It doesn't make sense!'

'And there are babies born every minute,' said Joshua.

'But this is a wonderful baby,' Reuben insisted. 'The Saviour of the world… that's what the voice said. It's a miracle!'

'Well, I don't want to see any miracles,' said Joshua firmly. 'I don't believe in them. You've been asleep, young Reuben, and having a bad dream.' With that he lay down and closed his eyes.

'Perhaps I have,' said Reuben doubtfully. 'The voice said something about going to Bethlehem…' He looked across the field, and that was when he discovered that a sheep was missing.

By now, the small sheep was far away. The going had been hard and the sheep was tired and thirsty. She stopped and looked around. Below her lay a pool of clear, still water. Above her, the sky was black, with a mass of white stars.

Everywhere was very quiet and very still.

She clambered down the bank and bent her head to drink. She could see stars reflected in the still water. She could see white, frost-covered hills. She could see her glittering eyes. But she could not see her face. Where there should have been a reflection of her face in the dark waters of the pool, she could see – nothing. For a long while she stared, then lifted her head.

So that's why I'm different, she thought. Now I know.

She turned to go but her foot slipped and she fell into the pool. Her legs became tangled in thick weeds.

'Help!' she called in fright. 'Help! Ba-aa!'

The flock grumbled as the shepherds drove them through the gap in the stone wall.

'It's a bit much taking us on a march at this time of the night,' said the first sheep.

'Who cares if *that* sheep's gone missing, anyway?' said the second sheep.

'Good riddance, I say,' said the third sheep.

'Who'd want to steal her?' asked the first sheep, sourly.

'Perhaps,' said a fourth sheep quietly, 'perhaps she just went off because we've been unkind to her.'

They looked at one another and fell silent.

As the shepherds drove their flock across the fields in search

of the lost sheep, the small, lonely sheep stopped struggling. She was very cold and just wanted to sleep. But, for one last time, she cried out, 'Baa-aa… Baa-aa… Help me…!'

And it was that cry that brought the shepherds running to the pool.

'She needs warmth,' said Reuben, wrapping her in his cloak.

'There's a stable over there,' said Elias.

So Reuben carried the small sheep to the stable. The door was open. Light and warmth streamed out. As Reuben entered, the small sheep stirred in his arms and opened her eyes. She saw the shepherds and the sheep staring at her. They looked worried and concerned.

They saved me, she thought. Perhaps they do want me, after all. A great warmth began to spread through her.

Then she saw the baby, lying in the straw-filled crib. She jumped out of Reuben's arms and ran across the floor. The baby held out his arms to welcome her – the small black sheep, lonely no longer.

The Animals' Christmas

There was a terrible traffic jam at the crossroads in the town of Bethlehem. The ox, tired after his hard day's work in the fields, snorted crossly. When he finally arrived at his stable he was in a bad mood.

'I don't know what's happening, I really don't,' he grumbled, as he came through the door. 'The town's gone mad! Do you know, it took me half an hour to get here from the field? And the noise! Dreadful…' the ox stopped and he stared round the stable. 'Here – what's going on?'

A donkey and two cows stared back at him.

'What are you doing here?' the ox demanded. 'This is *my* stable!'

'Sorry,' said one of the cows. 'There's nowhere else for us to go.'

'What do you mean, nowhere for you to go?' repeated the ox. 'Of course there is. The whole town's full of stables, half empty most of them!'

'My master's been round everywhere. This is the last stable with any room to spare.'

The ox's companion pushed his nose over the edge of his stall. 'What's going on in the town?' he asked quietly.

'Yes,' said one of the cows. 'What *is* going on? Why is Bethlehem so popular all of a sudden? It's not as if it's a holiday resort or a city.'

'I think it's because of the census,' said the donkey.

'What's that?'

'The Romans want to count all the people, so everyone has to go back to the place where they were born.'

'It still doesn't explain what you're all doing in *my* stable,' said the first ox, stubbornly.

'Yes it does,' said the donkey. 'The town's full, so we've been asked to share.'

Just then the stable door burst open.

'Oh close that door, for goodness' sake,' said an owl, calling down from her perch high up in the rafters. 'There's a terrible draught!'

A goat stood just inside the door. 'Sorry,' she bleated.

'I suppose you think you can share my stable tonight,' said the ox.

'Yes please,' said the goat.

'Well you've got another think coming,' said the ox, lowering his head dangerously. 'There's no room.'

'There's plenty of room,' said the goat.

'I don't care if there's all the room in the world!' the ox bellowed. 'This is *my* stable!'

'It's not *your* stable,' said a mouse, running across the

floor. 'I live here as well.'

'So do I,' hooted the owl.

'It's my home too,' whispered a spider from the middle of her web.

'What I mean is, I won't have strangers coming in!' said the ox crossly.

'Just as well I'm not a stranger then,' said the innkeeper's cat, jumping in through the window. The mouse squeaked and ran for cover.

The stable door opened once more and a horse came in.

'Shut that door!' shouted the owl.

The horse looked around the stable. 'Well really,' he complained. 'This is not the kind of accommodation I'm used to.'

'In that case, why don't you go?' said the ox rudely.

'And close the door behind you,' added the owl.

'I'm used to a stall by myself,' said the horse, 'with good fresh hay and a warm blanket to keep out the cold.'

'We're all stuck here for the night,' said the goat, 'so we'd better make the best of it.'

'*I'm* not prepared to make the best of it,' said the ox firmly. 'You seem to forget this is *my* stable!'

'And mine,' said the quiet ox. 'But I don't mind. It's nice to talk to other animals. You can get a bit boring at times.'

'Boring!' gasped the first ox. 'Me? Why you… you…' He lowered his head to charge.

'Now stop that!' said one of the cows in a firm voice. 'I don't like violence. It upsets me and as I'm expecting a baby…'

'That'll make it even more crowded,' giggled the goat.

'If you think this is crowded, you should see the inn!' said the cat. 'At least two to a bed. And the noise! I've come here for a bit of peace and quiet.'

'It doesn't seem like there's going to be much peace in here tonight,' said the donkey, 'and as for quiet…'

'FOR THE LAST TIME, WILL YOU ALL GET OUT!' shouted the ox.

'NO!' the other animals roared back. The cows mooed, the donkey brayed, the goat bleated, the owl hooted, and the mouse brought his excited family in to watch the fun.

'I wish you wouldn't always get so angry,' the quiet ox said to his friend.

But the first ox was not listening. Head down, hooves pawing the ground, he charged. Everyone moved out of the way and the ox would have hit his head against the stable door if it had not suddenly opened. Unable to stop himself, he rushed straight out of the stable, across the courtyard, and landed head first in a large pile of hay.

The animals cheered.

A shabby-looking donkey, patiently waiting to come inside, looked round. 'What was that?' he asked.

'Just my friend,' said the quiet ox. 'Take no notice. I expect you want shelter for the night.'

'Yes please,' said the donkey. 'I do. And my master and mistress too. We've travelled a long way and we're all tired.'

The donkey entered the stable. On his back was a young girl, and a man followed on foot.

The animals looked at the new arrivals.

'Have you come far?' asked the cow.

'From Nazareth,' said the donkey.

The man helped the girl from the donkey's back.

'Oh look,' said the cow, pleased. 'She's expecting a baby, just like me!'

'Ahh,' said the owl. 'I do like babies. I've been quite lonely since mine have grown up and flown the nest.'

The man gathered some straw for a bed and the girl lay down. She smiled up at him, then closed her eyes.

There was a furious pounding on the door.

35

'That'll be the ox,' sighed the goat. 'I wouldn't let him in if I were you.'

'But it's his stable as well as mine,' said the quiet ox.

The ox burst in, then stopped in amazement. 'What on earth's going on now?'

'I think,' said the owl, 'that the girl is having a baby. Do close the door, and try not to get in the way.'

'Humans?' spluttered the ox. 'In *my* stable?' He shook his head. 'Well, I'm speechless!'

'Thank goodness for that,' said the goat.

It was peaceful in the stable as the baby was born. The only sounds to be heard were the breathing of the animals, the odd shuffling and rustles of straw, and the flutter of wings as the owl flew to and fro.

At last, the baby gave a cry. The animals drew near the rough crib in which he lay. The baby opened his eyes and the animals sank to their knees.

'This,' said the cow, 'is no ordinary baby.'

Everyone was silent, even the ox. But soon the peace was broken by a loud banging. The door burst open and in walked three shepherds, followed by their sheep.

'Well really!' exclaimed the ox. 'They barge in without a "by your leave" or a "would you mind?" Some people have no manners!'

But he no longer sounded cross. Neither did the owl, who ruffled her feathers as she said, 'Close that door, we don't want the baby to catch cold!'

The Confused Camels

The wind was blowing hard across the desert, whirling sand into the faces of the three camels and their riders. They had travelled a long way and were very tired. They went in single file, the largest camel leading, the smallest at the back. The camels were being ridden by three wise men following a bright new star in the sky.

The largest camel was being ridden by Melchior, the middle camel was being ridden by Caspar and the smallest camel was being ridden by Balthazar. Each camel was carrying precious gifts of gold, frankincense and myrrh.

Caspar's camel suddenly sneezed. 'It's all this sand,' he complained.

'What do you expect in the desert?' asked Melchior's camel, disagreeably.

The camels and their riders plodded on. The sun set quickly and soon it was quite dark. Melchior's camel stopped suddenly and Caspar's camel bumped into him.

'Whatever do you think you're doing, stopping like that?' he hissed angrily.

'Quiet!' said Melchior's camel. 'I'm thinking.'

'Thinking! Huh! I'm beginning to think it wasn't such a good idea to set off on this journey in the first place,' said Caspar's camel. 'And I'm beginning to wonder whether we'll ever see this king – if there is a king.'

'A wise camel should never have doubts,' said Melchior's camel. 'My master is searching for the baby who is a king, so he can give him a wonderful present. And I, being the oldest and wisest of the camels, shall carry him there.'

'Well, I think you've got us lost,' said Caspar's camel.

'I'm following the new star,' Melchior's camel said.

'Where is this star then?'

The three camels looked up at the sky. But nothing could be seen through the swirling of dust and sand.

'I vote we stop here for the night,' said Caspar's camel.

'There's no question of a vote,' said Melchior's camel. 'I am in charge of this journey and what I say goes.'

'What do you think?' Caspar's camel asked the smallest camel.

'Me?' The smallest camel was startled. No one ever asked for his opinion. 'Oh, I think we should do what our masters want.'

'In the desert, we, the camels, are in charge,' Melchior's camel said grandly. 'Our masters only *think* they are in charge.'

With that, he turned and began to walk away into the night. Grumbling and complaining, Caspar's camel followed. The smallest camel silently brought up the rear.

At last the storm blew itself out. The clouds parted and a starry sky was seen. The leading camel stopped once more.

'I suppose you're thinking again,' said Caspar's camel, sourly.

'That's right.'

All three camels looked up and the smallest camel gasped.

'I've never seen so many stars before.'

'That's just because you've not been around for very long,' said Melchior's camel, in a kind but superior voice. 'When you've seen as many starlit skies as I have you soon learn to travel by them. Why, I can read the night sky like a map.'

'If it's all so easy, why don't you get on with it?' complained Caspar's camel. 'As far as I'm concerned, I'll be glad to find this king and get home. A bit of shade under a palm tree and a nice waterhole would do me very well.'

The smallest camel said nothing at all, but thought longingly of water, shade and a long, long rest. This was his first big journey into the desert.

Despite his talk, Melchior's camel was confused by the sight of so many stars. Some were bright and some were dim, some were large and some were small, but no single star seemed bigger and brighter than the others. But he was not going to admit it, so they set off once more.

On the third day Melchior's camel began to go slower and slower.

'You know what?' Caspar's camel asked, looking round. 'We've been here before.'

'Rubbish,' said Melchior's camel.

'I recognize that hill over there.'

'Everything shifts and changes in the desert,' said Melchior's camel. 'It's a well-known fact that you can think you're going round in circles when really…'

'You *are* going round in circles,' said Caspar's camel. He stopped and so did the smallest camel.

'You're right,' Melchior's camel admitted unhappily. 'We *are* going round in circles.'

Caspar's camel was furious. 'Fine kind of leader you've turned out to be,' he said. 'Get out of the way – I'm in charge now!'

He turned and headed back the way they had just come.

With a sigh Melchior's camel fell into second place and, as usual, the smallest camel followed behind.

That night the sky was clear and inky black and studded with thousands upon thousands of stars.

'See,' said Caspar's camel. 'I was right. There's the star. We'll soon find this baby king.'

The smallest camel said nothing and they all walked on. But as he walked, the smallest camel could not help thinking that the brightest star was not in front of them, but somewhere behind them.

After another day and a night, the three camels and their riders came to a small town.

'This is it,' said Caspar's camel.

Thankfully, the three wise men climbed off their camels and went in search of food, rest and the baby king.

The three camels also rested and drank greedily from the waterhole. There were other camels there and they began to talk. As they talked, Caspar's camel's face fell. For the other camels were saying that this was not the town they were seeking at all.

'But I've been following the new star!' Caspar's camel insisted.

'Sorry, you must have been following an old one,' said the other camels.

The three wise men came back and the two oldest camels looked at the smallest one.

'It's up to you,' they said.

'Me?' said the smallest camel. 'But I'm not old or wise or well travelled like you.'

'That doesn't seem to count for anything,' said Melchior's camel.

'Not in the desert,' added Caspar's camel.

So they set off, this time with the smallest camel in front.
Night fell and the smallest camel looked up at the velvety black
sky with its mass of silver stars.

The stars twinkled and gleamed. Some of them were large

and some were small, but none was brighter than the others.

Oh dear, thought the smallest camel. I don't know which is the right star, but I do want to find the baby king. My master's gift isn't precious, like gold or frankincense, because he's a poor man. But he paid all he could for the myrrh and he's come a long way to give it to the baby.

As he was thinking these thoughts, one star, low on the horizon, began to glow. As the smallest camel watched, it seemed to glow brighter and bigger than all the rest.

Slowly, at first, and then with more confidence, the smallest camel began walking towards this star, and the other two camels followed. On and on they trudged, right across the desert. Melchior on his camel, Caspar on his, with Balthazar's small camel surely and confidently leading the way.

At last the star came to rest above a stable in a small town. The camels and their riders rode in through the gates.

The wise men entered the stable carrying their precious gifts
of gold, frankincense and myrrh, and laid them before the baby.
The camels followed their masters and, as the smallest camel
knelt in the straw, he could have sworn that the baby looked
at him and smiled.

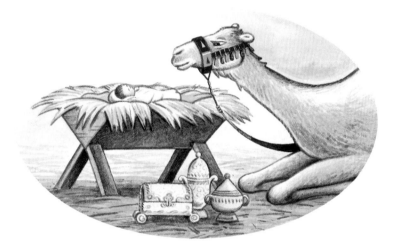